PLANET OF THE APES

Leo's Logbook: A Captain's Days in Captivity

Benjamin Athens

based on the motion picture screenplay

written by William Broyles, Jr.,

and Lawrence Konner & Mark D. Rosenthal

HarperEntertainment
An Imprint of HarperCollinsPublishers

To Mike and Steve,
for never driving me ape

 HarperEntertainment

An Imprint of HarperCollins*Publishers*
10 East 53rd Street, New York, NY 10022-5299

HarperCollins books are available at special quantity discounts for bulk purchases for sales promotions, premiums, or fund-raising. For information please call or write: Special Markets Department, HarperCollins Publishers Inc., 10 East 53rd Street, New York, NY 10022.

ISBN 0-06-093769-6

HarperCollins®, ®, and HarperEntertainment™ are trademarks of HarperCollins Publishers Inc.

Cover design by Victor Cagno

Interior design by Harry Nolan

First printing: August 2001

Printed in the United States of America

Visit HarperEntertainment on the World Wide Web at http://www.harpercollins.com

10 9 8 7 6 5 4 3 2 1

"I am Captain Leo Davidson of the United States Air Force."

Captain's Log

I don't know who is going to read this—maybe no one. But I have to write down what has happened to me. It is unbelievable . . . and true.

I am Captain Leo Davidson of the United States Air Force. In the past few days, I have seen things no man of my time has ever seen before. I have gone to a place that cannot possibly exist—but it does. This is my story.

The USAF Oberon and Its Mission

A long time ago, a chimpanzee was sent into space as an experiment. We wanted to see what would happen to the ape before we sent people into space. The chimp didn't have to do anything. He just sat there as the rocket went up and the pod came back down to Earth. Everything went according to plan. The path to human exploration of space was cleared.

Now it's the next century—2029 to be exact. We no longer plan to walk on the moon or map out Mars—we've done that already. We're looking to take the next great steps—to chart the great unknown and explore the strange things that happen there.

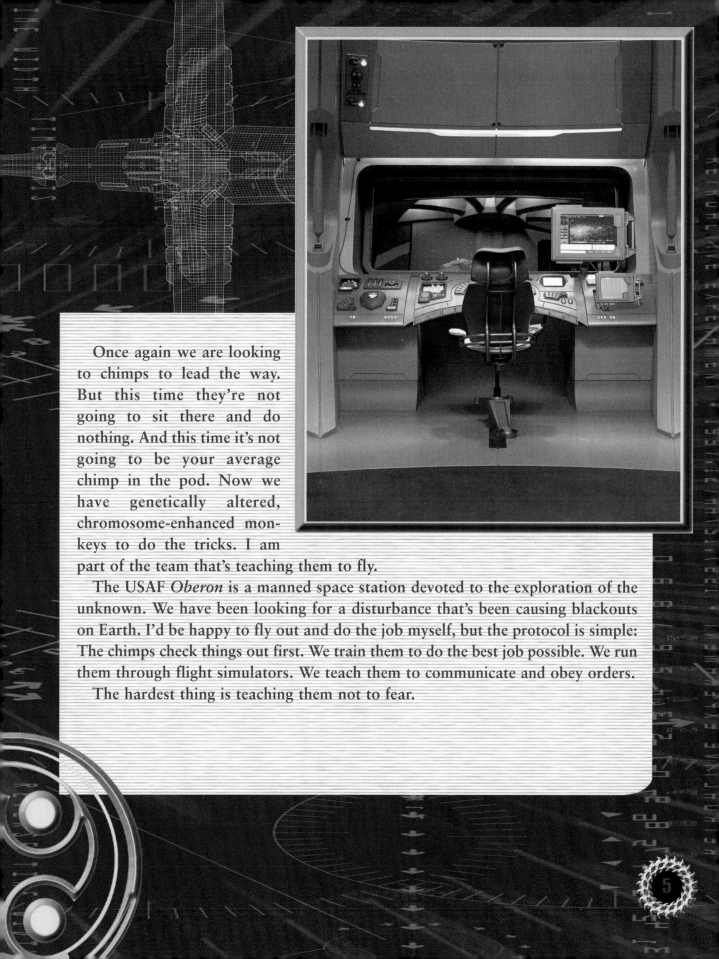

Once again we are looking to chimps to lead the way. But this time they're not going to sit there and do nothing. And this time it's not going to be your average chimp in the pod. Now we have genetically altered, chromosome-enhanced monkeys to do the tricks. I am part of the team that's teaching them to fly.

The USAF *Oberon* is a manned space station devoted to the exploration of the unknown. We have been looking for a disturbance that's been causing blackouts on Earth. I'd be happy to fly out and do the job myself, but the protocol is simple: The chimps check things out first. We train them to do the best job possible. We run them through flight simulators. We teach them to communicate and obey orders.

The hardest thing is teaching them not to fear.

The Crew

The crew of the *Oberon* was chosen from among the most experienced fliers, scientists, and astronauts in the United States Air Force. My fellow crew members are:

LT. COL. GRACE ALEXANDER: Grace is our chief medical officer and zoologist, which means she spends a lot of time with primates. I think she likes it that way. She says that humans—especially men—can be a drag. Chimps are easier to deal with, since she always knows where she stands with them. I certainly don't know where I stand with Grace. Sometimes I think she really likes me. And sometimes I think she'd really like to turn me into an orangutan.

COMMANDER KARL VASICH: Commander Vasich is the flight chief of our mission—something he rarely lets us forget. He's stubborn, blunt, and determined to succeed. Since I am pretty much all those things, too, sometimes we get on each other's case. I have to respect him, even if I don't listen to him all the time. He likes to play by the rules. I like to see how far they'll stretch.

SPECIALIST HANSEN: Hansen is our technology geek. It's up to him to translate all the beeps and flashes on our digital screens into the language of space. He's the one who monitors the monitors and looks for the signs of the unknown. Although I'm sure he sleeps, I've never seen him do it.

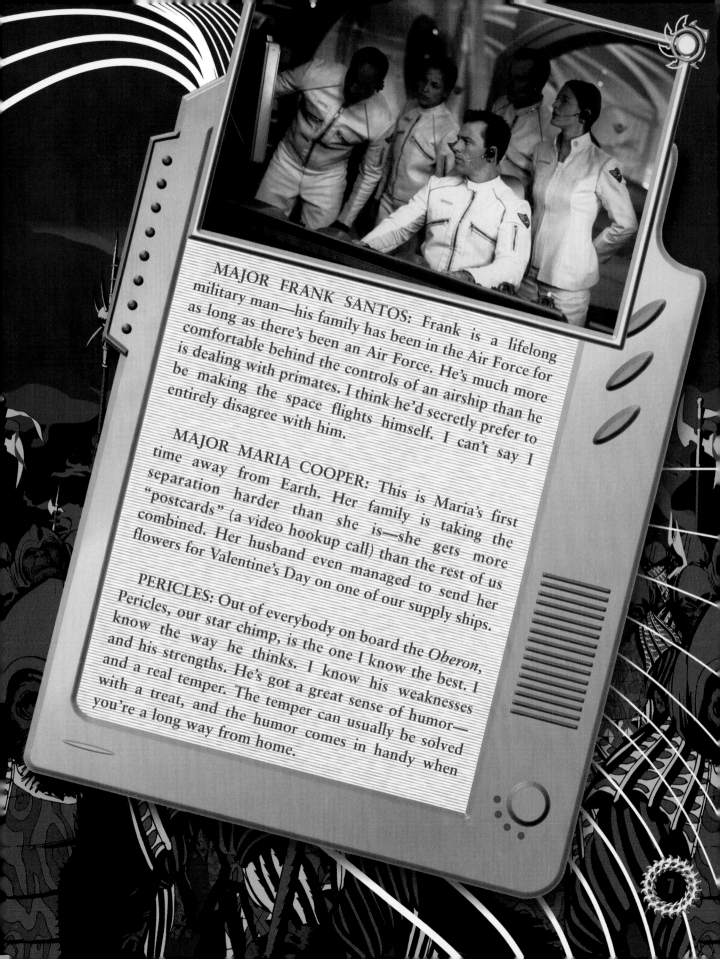

MAJOR FRANK SANTOS: Frank is a lifelong military man—his family has been in the Air Force for as long as there's been an Air Force. He's much more comfortable behind the controls of an airship than he is dealing with primates. I think he'd secretly prefer to be making the space flights himself. I can't say I entirely disagree with him.

MAJOR MARIA COOPER: This is Maria's first time away from Earth. Her family is taking the separation harder than she is—she gets more "postcards" (a video hookup call) than the rest of us combined. Her husband even managed to send her flowers for Valentine's Day on one of our supply ships.

PERICLES: Out of everybody on board the *Oberon*, Pericles, our star chimp, is the one I know the best. I know the way he thinks. I know his weaknesses and his strengths. He's got a great sense of humor—and a real temper. The temper can usually be solved with a treat, and the humor comes in handy when you're a long way from home.

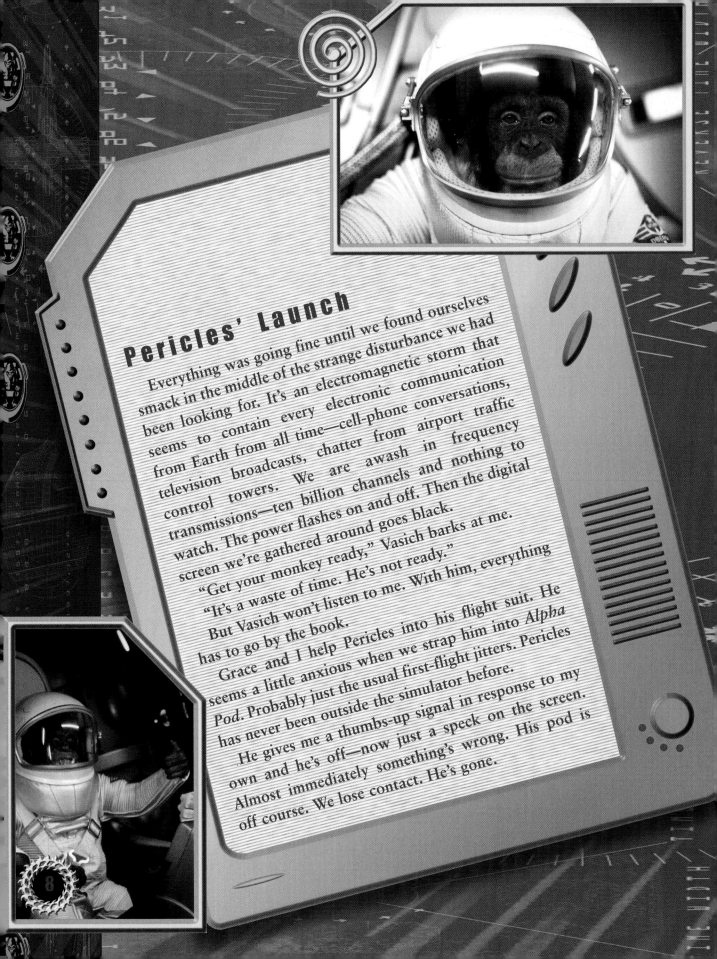

Pericles' Launch

Everything was going fine until we found ourselves smack in the middle of the strange disturbance we had been looking for. It's an electromagnetic storm that seems to contain every electronic communication from Earth from all time—cell-phone conversations, television broadcasts, chatter from airport traffic control towers. We are awash in frequency transmissions—ten billion channels and nothing to watch. The power flashes on and off. Then the digital screen we're gathered around goes black.

"Get your monkey ready," Vasich barks at me.

"It's a waste of time. He's not ready."

But Vasich won't listen to me. With him, everything has to go by the book.

Grace and I help Pericles into his flight suit. He seems a little anxious when we strap him into *Alpha* Pod. Probably just the usual first-flight jitters. Pericles has never been outside the simulator before.

He gives me a thumbs-up signal in response to my own and he's off—now just a speck on the screen. Almost immediately something's wrong. His pod is off course. We lose contact. He's gone.

You should never send a monkey to do a man's job.

"I'll run some sequences in *Delta Pod*," I say out loud. "See if I can figure out what he did wrong." My plan is to go after him, but I can't tell that to Vasich.

The instant I launch, an order comes from him for me to return to the *Oberon*. No way. Now I've got Pericles' pod in my sight and I've got to get to him, guide him home. Light glitters around our pods. Vasich continues to shout, "Abort mission, return to ship," until I hear nothing but static.

All of a sudden I lose sight of the *Alpha Pod* as well as all contact with the *Oberon*. I'm rocked by a tidal wave of light. My system shuts down . . . no life support. I can't breathe.

Then the control monitor explodes into full color. The power's back on. I'm going to make it! But then the clock goes haywire—flashes dates thousands of years in the future, then thousands of years in the past. The pod accelerates and I have absolutely no control. Faster . . . faster. I see land approaching. The pod is on fire. It crashes through treetops, then smacks into the water.

Somehow I manage to get out of there, eject underwater, tear off my flight suit, and swim to the surface.

I see nothing but jungle. Where am I?

A Strange Planet

Cut and bruised, I run into the jungle for cover. I hear strange cries and brutal roars and muffled voices. Hidden behind leaves and branches, I arm myself with a rock.

An older man and a young woman burst onto the path in front of me. They are dirty, with strange markings on their faces. It is clear they are running for their lives. The woman knocks the rock from my hand and moves on. The man shoves me aside to get by. From within the jungle I hear the eerie metallic sound of bells. The branches all around me shake as dark, shadowy figures move closer.

I rush after the humans. The cries grow louder. The bells are closer. Suddenly I hear a growl right by my ear. I look up and find myself face-to-face with a fierce gorilla. But this is no ordinary gorilla. This gorilla wears full armor and a helmet.

What kind of strange place is this? I grab a branch to defend myself, but the ape snaps it out of my hands and sends me flying. After crashing hard on the ground, I stagger to my feet. The jungle is swarming with other apes in armor attacking the humans.

> "Take your stinking hand off me, you dirty human!"
> — Attar

It's like a nightmare come true, where all the things you know can't be real actually exist. Apes don't ride horses, but there are apes riding horses surrounding me. Humans are supposed to be hunters, not prey. But these humans are clearly being hunted and captured. I could be next.

I knock an ape off its horse and try to flee. Before I can even mount the horse, another ape grabs me from above and tosses me back to the ground. The apes bind my wrists and push me into a crowd of humans. Then another ape arrives, this one in a glittering gold uniform.

In a lightning flash, the golden ape grabs me by the hair—and speaks! In English! "This one looked at me!" he roars.

I must be going crazy. It's not possible.

"He won't do it again," another ape says. He whacks me on the head and I see nothing more.

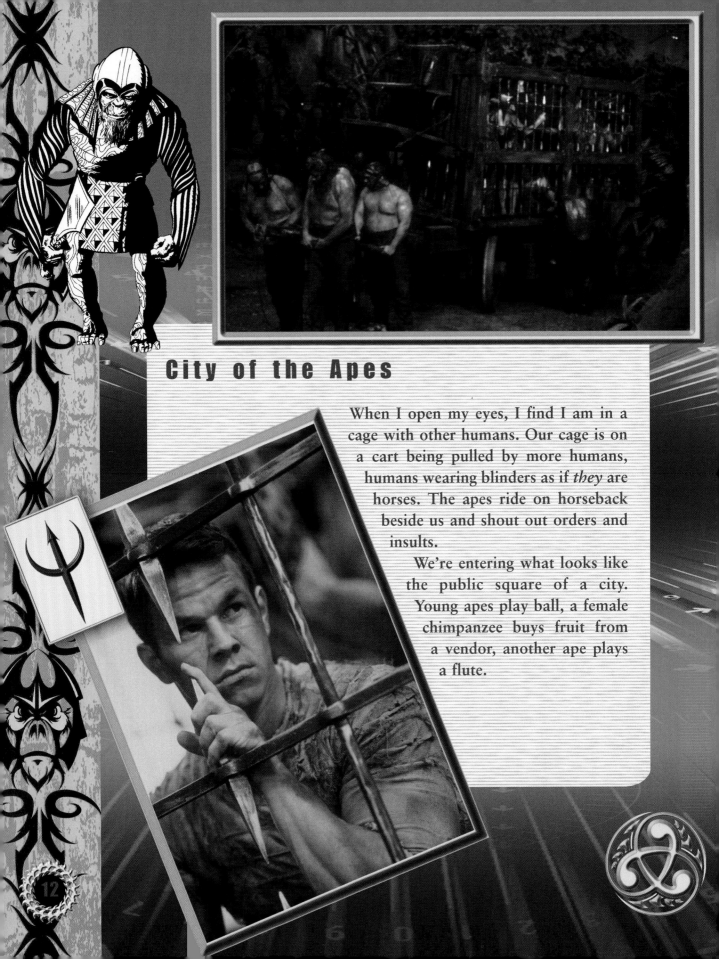

City of the Apes

When I open my eyes, I find I am in a cage with other humans. Our cage is on a cart being pulled by more humans, humans wearing blinders as if *they* are horses. The apes ride on horseback beside us and shout out orders and insults.

We're entering what looks like the public square of a city. Young apes play ball, a female chimpanzee buys fruit from a vendor, another ape plays a flute.

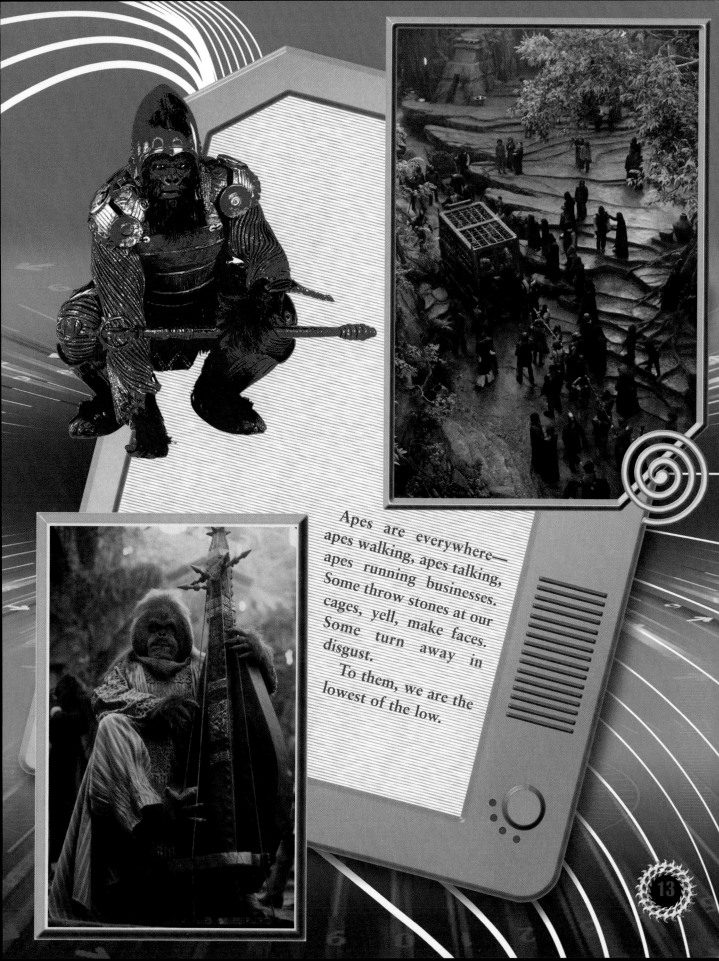

Apes are everywhere—apes walking, apes talking, apes running businesses. Some throw stones at our cages, yell, make faces. Some turn away in disgust.

To them, we are the lowest of the low.

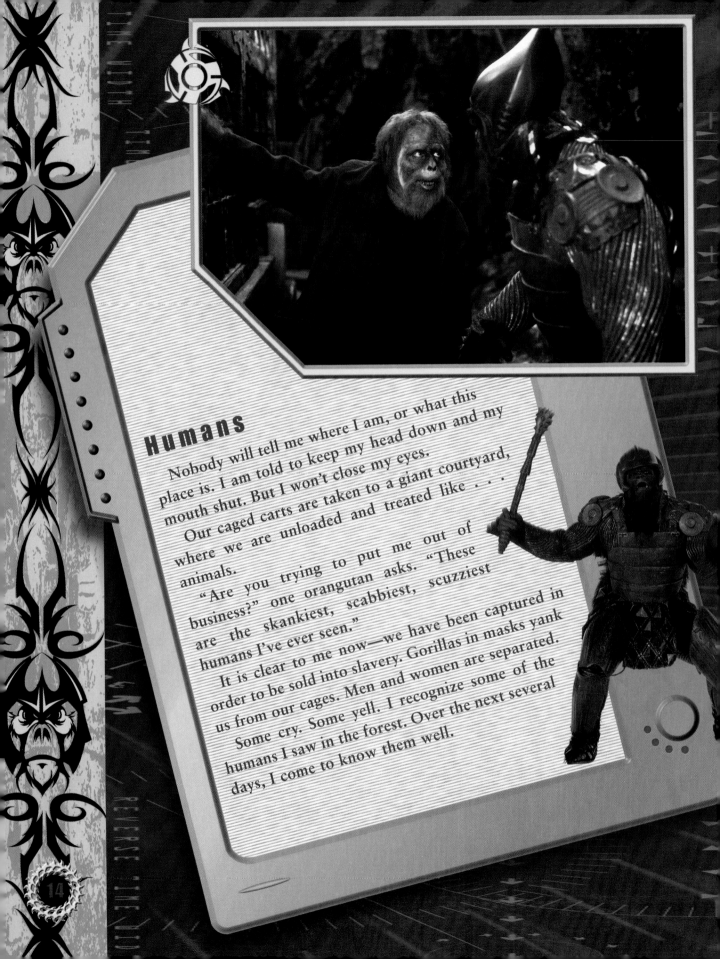

Humans

Nobody will tell me where I am, or what this place is. I am told to keep my head down and my mouth shut. But I won't close my eyes.

Our caged carts are taken to a giant courtyard, where we are unloaded and treated like . . . animals.

"Are you trying to put me out of business?" one orangutan asks. "These are the skankiest, scabbiest, scuzziest humans I've ever seen."

It is clear to me now—we have been captured in order to be sold into slavery. Gorillas in masks yank us from our cages. Men and women are separated. Some cry. Some yell. I recognize some of the humans I saw in the forest. Over the next several days, I come to know them well.

> "These are the skankiest, scabbiest, scuzziest humans I've ever seen."

Karubi

Karubi is a leader in the purest sense of the word—he tries to find the best way for us to go forward. He leads by example. He leads with wisdom.

He is not a commander, because he rarely commands. He is not reckless in his power. He values the bigger picture over a single action.

Karubi was the first human I encountered, the one I almost attacked with a rock. I am very glad I didn't. He was leading his people in a raid on an orchard—cut off from other food supplies, they had to steal in order to live. He has been running all his life, and now he's been captured at last.

Daena

Strong and beautiful, Daena is Karubi's daughter and nobody's fool. She feels the same things toward the apes that the apes feel toward her—anger, distrust, and loathing. She has always lived on the outside of the ape world. She's never had a place to call home. Just like her father, she's lived her whole life on the move. I don't know what happened to Daena's mother—but I suspect it wasn't good. Daena's anger is fierce.

Gunnar

Gunnar is stocky and strong and has a good heart. But even he is afraid of the apes. Given the chance, though, I'm sure he would fight for freedom . . . at any cost.

Birn

The teenage Birn may be young, but he's a fighter. He is all instinct and action. He moves with the swiftness of a cheetah, and there is an intense wildness to him. He's not afraid to resist the apes the way the other humans are. He's the only one who will look me in the eye and he believes strongly in what we are doing. He looks up to me and I'm certain he would do anything I ask.

"Someday, if humans are even remembered, they will be known for what they really are—weak and stupid." — Thade

The Apes

Now that I've been here for what seems like forever, I've learned the names and positions of the most important apes.

THADE: Thade is the ruthless general of the ape army. He doesn't like to be threatened, and he makes his own rules. The others seem to love him for it. He inspires a sense of glory in them. I'm told he is a direct descendant of Semos, an ape god all the apes worship. It is clear he wants to be worshiped, too. He's halfway there, but he needs to enslave—or eliminate—every last human. He wants to have absolute power.

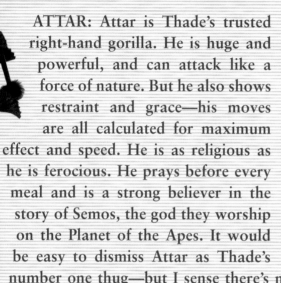

ATTAR: Attar is Thade's trusted right-hand gorilla. He is huge and powerful, and can attack like a force of nature. But he also shows restraint and grace—his moves are all calculated for maximum effect and speed. He is as religious as he is ferocious. He prays before every meal and is a strong believer in the story of Semos, the god they worship on the Planet of the Apes. It would be easy to dismiss Attar as Thade's number one thug—but I sense there's more than monkey-see, monkey-do going on here. Attar has a mind of his own. His faith runs to higher things than Thade.

LIMBO: This slimy orangutan is the most successful slave trader in the City of the Apes. He calls us skanky, scuzzy humans, but he's the biggest scum I've ever met. He sells humans as if we were car parts—we are merely a product to him. He used to hack off humans' limbs when they misbehaved, but he stopped because the slaves are more valuable when they are whole. Money is the most important thing in Limbo's world. His greed overshadows everything else.

"Hey, I do the job that nobody else wants, spending all day with these dumb, dirty beasts."
—Limbo

Apes and Their Humans

Back on Earth, I used to hear stories of men who were taken as prisoners of war. They were tortured and beaten and starved. Now I know how it feels.

Right before my eyes, Daena is dragged roughly to a wooden pole. The apes bare her shoulder and scorch her with a branding iron. Even though her father cries out, she doesn't flinch.

This brand marks all human slaves.

I will not let them do this to me.

When two apes approach, I kick the iron out of their hands.

"Do I have to do everything myself?" Limbo asks with a sigh. He reaches for the iron. But before he can grasp it, another ape grabs it and hurls it aside. I cannot believe it. An ape standing up for us—the slaves!

"What's disgusting is the way we treat humans. It demeans us as well as them."
— Ari

Ari

The ape who tried to protect me is Ari. Ari believes in human rights. She cannot stand the way humans are treated on her world. For her actions, she is called a human lover and a bleeding heart. Other apes—even her friends—do not like the things she does. Some of them would like to destroy her. Luckily she comes from a very powerful family . . . and is not afraid to speak her mind or her heart.

"I cannot stand idly by while humans are being mistreated, tortured . . ." she now tells Limbo. She runs over to one of the women's cages and opens the lock. Before anyone can escape, a massive gorilla stands in the way.

Ari won't give up. "If you want me to stop, give up your bloody business," she says. "They're not dumb. They can be taught to live with us. I'm going to prove it."

The apes are now fully distracted, mumbling angrily and shuffling their feet. It's time to make my move. I whip a chain around one of the handlers feet and steal his spear. I need to get close to Ari to ask her something. I jump toward her and hold the spear to her neck so none of the other apes will come closer.

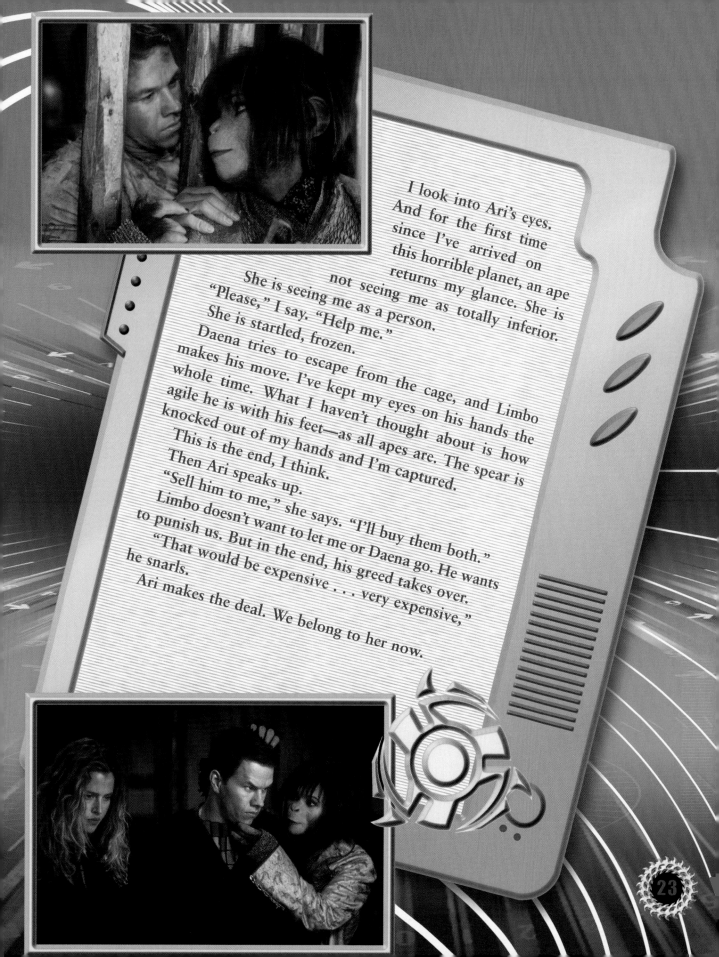

I look into Ari's eyes. And for the first time since I've arrived on this horrible planet, an ape returns my glance. She is not seeing me as totally inferior. She is seeing me as a person.

"Please," I say. "Help me."

She is startled, frozen.

Daena tries to escape from the cage, and Limbo makes his move. I've kept my eyes on his hands the whole time. What I haven't thought about is how agile he is with his feet—as all apes are. The spear is knocked out of my hands and I'm captured.

This is the end, I think.

Then Ari speaks up.

"Sell him to me," she says. "I'll buy them both."

Limbo doesn't want to let me or Daena go. He wants to punish us. But in the end, his greed takes over.

"That would be expensive . . . very expensive," he snarls.

Ari makes the deal. We belong to her now.

Ari's House

Ari's father, Sandar, is a senator—a very powerful ape with a very large house to match. The house of a rich and powerful ape is much like the house of a rich and powerful human—it contains many rooms, some of which are only for decoration. Possessions are on display to impress visitors. Servants must remain silent and stay out of the way.

Sandar's Servants

Daena and I are not the only servants in Sandar and Ari's house. There are three others.

Krull, a hulking silverback gorilla, is in charge of all the servants. Unlike Ari, he is not a fan of humans. He used to be a general in the army until he opposed Thade. Then Sandar took him in. It's clear he will do whatever it takes to protect Ari.

Tival is a "house human." He has been "trained" to behave inside Sandar's house and is well groomed and neatly dressed in robes, the attire of all servants.

Bon is also a house human. She is an expert seamstress, who creates dazzling clothes for Ari.

Daena: What tribe do you come from?

Leo: It's called the United States Air Force. And I'm going back to it.

The Dinner Party

There is a big dinner party that night at Sandar's. I am amazed at how much it is like a high-society dinner party on Earth—the same meaningless chatter, the same disregard for the servants. But we see and hear everything. Even as the other apes make fun of and threaten humans, Ari stands up for us. She says humans have souls. And as she says that, I realize that she has a soul, too. I don't understand. How did the apes ever get like this? And how can some be so good, and others so evil?

One of the guests at the dinner is Nado, an old friend of Ari's father who has devoted his whole life to politics . . . and has become very wealthy in the process. He sees no reason to change things.

Nova is Nado's much younger wife. She spends a fortune grooming herself and she's always worried about having a bad hair day. In her case it means the hair on her face.

Sandar clearly cares about his daughter. He is constantly bailing her out of the trouble she gets in by trying to improve life for the humans. He also goes to considerable expense to pay for her impulses (such as buying new slaves, lucky for me). But he is not willing to go as far as she is in order to help the humans. Like his friend, Nado, he is too used to the way things are.

A chimp named Leeta is also at the party. She's Ari's best friend . . . but not her best ally. She can't understand why Ari has any feelings for the humans. She is constantly warning Ari not to get into any more trouble, and not to bother with her cause.

RULES FOR HUMANS

No talking.

No eye contact.

Obey all masters.

Question nothing.

Sleep in a cage.

Never try to escape.

Escape!

That night, after the party, I use a utensil stolen from the dinner table to pry open our cages. I want to make a quick escape, but Daena insists we return to the slave pens to free her father first. Tival comes with us, but not Bon.

We sneak into Limbo's slave quarters and free Karubi, Birn, and Gunnar.

I think we might actually make a clean escape, but then we run into a bunch of young apes and they sound an alarm cry. If we hadn't been noticed before, we will be now.

We snake through the narrow streets trying not to be seen. I see two apes step out from the shadows. I take out my knife, prepared to attack. Then I realize it's only Ari and Krull.

"You're lucky I found you before they did," Ari says.

"Do not get involved with these humans," Krull warns.

But she's already involved. I can tell.

"Why did you save me?" I ask her. "Why did you take the chance?"

She might not know the reasons. But whatever they were, I hope they will save all of us again.

"When I was little I found a way to sneak outside the city walls, where no one could find me," she says. "I can lead you there."

"If you are caught, even your father won't be able to protect you," Krull tells her. But she's on our side. And Krull will not leave her. We continue on our way. The air is full of terrible roars. We are being hunted once again.

"Hurry," Karubi says to Daena, who seems unable to move. From the way he says it, she knows he is saying good-bye. He has a plan.

"No, Father!" she protests.

"Don't worry, I'll be right beside you," he replies. "Just like always."

He dashes out of the shadows to divert our enemies' attention. We take advantage of the time he's bought us and plunge on. Daena stumbles as we hear Karubi cry out. She wants to go back to him, but it is too late. There is no going back. Only forward.

Out of the City

We crawl through the cisterns and make it to the outside world. Daena is still shaken by her father's sacrifice. When Ari tries to console her, she lashes back. The tension grows.

The humans don't trust the apes. The apes don't trust the humans. I don't know who to trust. I just want to get back to my ship.

"Look how they pamper her," Gunnar grunts when Ari is offered fruit and water.

"I'm fine," Ari replies, pushing the food away.

"Apes are always fine . . . as long as you have humans to serve you," Daena snarls.

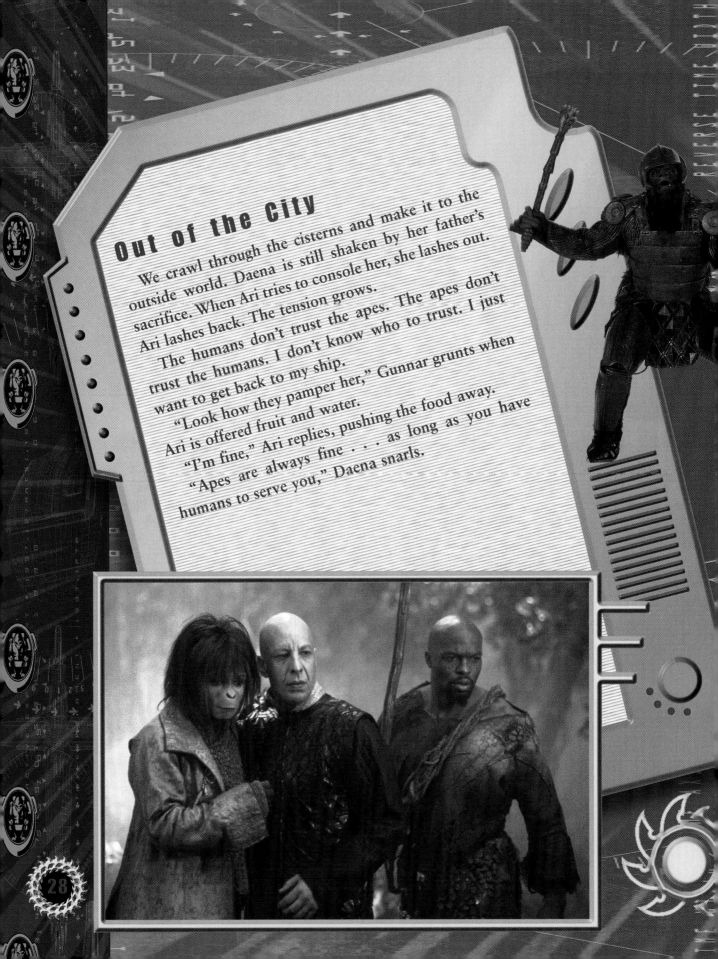

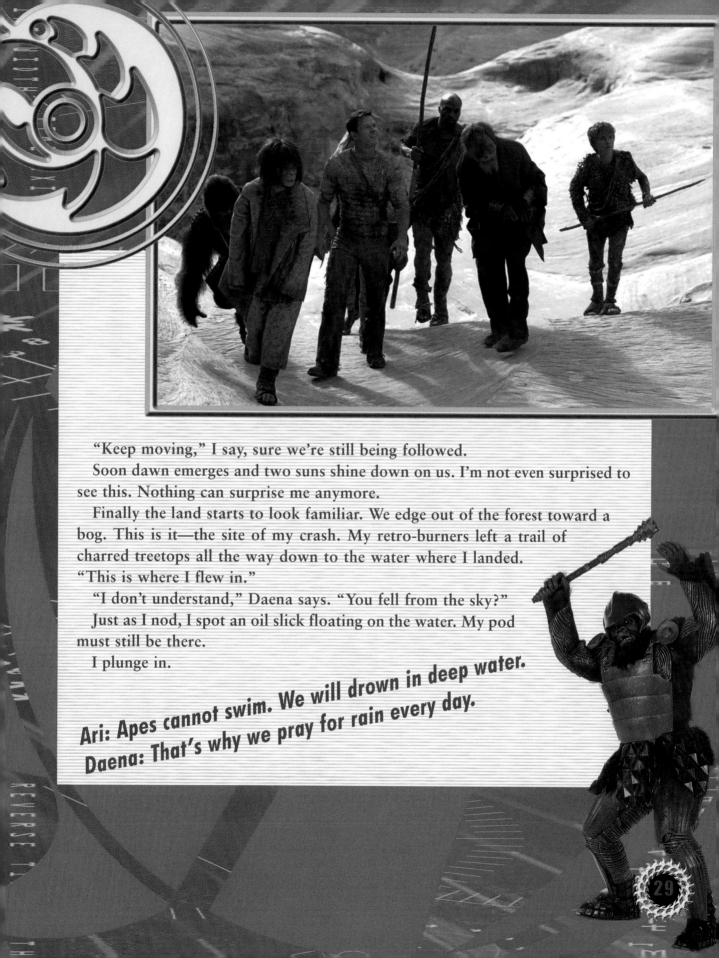

"Keep moving," I say, sure we're still being followed.

Soon dawn emerges and two suns shine down on us. I'm not even surprised to see this. Nothing can surprise me anymore.

Finally the land starts to look familiar. We edge out of the forest toward a bog. This is it—the site of my crash. My retro-burners left a trail of charred treetops all the way down to the water where I landed. "This is where I flew in."

"I don't understand," Daena says. "You fell from the sky?"

Just as I nod, I spot an oil slick floating on the water. My pod must still be there.

I plunge in.

Ari: Apes cannot swim. We will drown in deep water.
Daena: That's why we pray for rain every day.

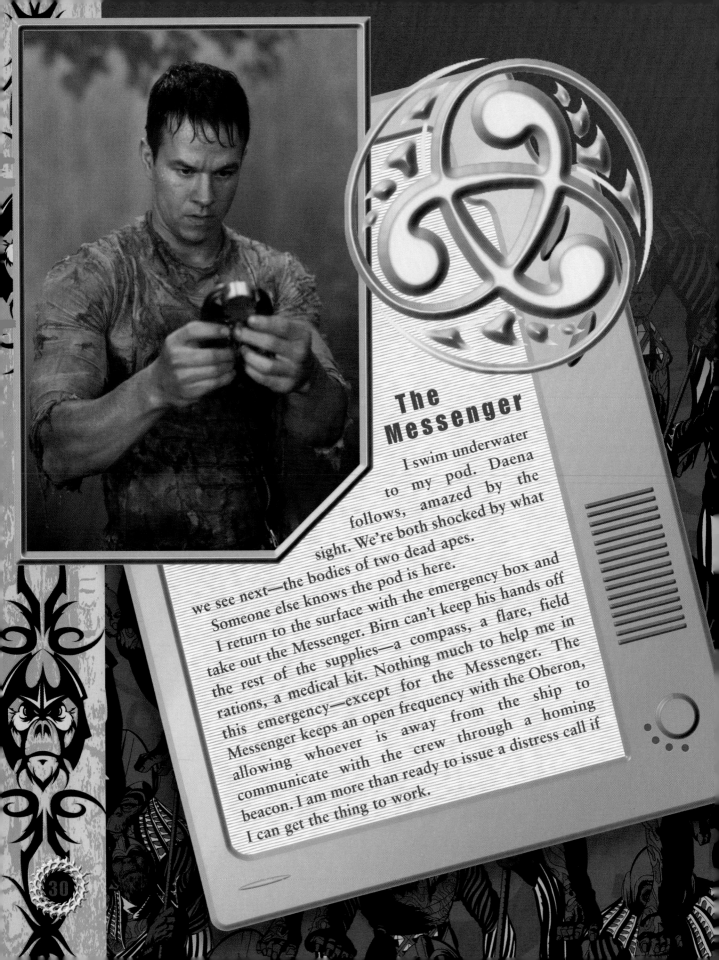

The Messenger

I swim underwater to my pod. Daena follows, amazed by the sight. We're both shocked by what we see next—the bodies of two dead apes. Someone else knows the pod is here.

I return to the surface with the emergency box and take out the Messenger. Birn can't keep his hands off the rest of the supplies—a compass, a flare, field rations, a medical kit. Nothing much to help me in this emergency—except for the Messenger. The Messenger keeps an open frequency with the Oberon, allowing whoever is away from the ship to communicate with the crew through a homing beacon. I am more than ready to issue a distress call if I can get the thing to work.

Tival: Your apes permit you to fly?
Leo: Our apes live in zoos. . . .
They do what we tell them.

The apes and humans all jump when the Messenger squawks to life with a beep.

I'm expecting the beacon to tell me that the ship is hovering somewhere above me in space. Instead, the beacon shows that the *Oberon* has already landed nearby.

They're here. I'm going home . . .

"You'd better warn them about the apes," Daena says.

"Better warn the apes about them," I reply.

We're in control now.

I have thirty-six hours to make a rendezvous.

Ari: What are these "zoos" you speak of? . . .
This word is unfamiliar.
Leo: Zoos are where you'll find our last few apes.
Krull: What happened to the rest of them?
Leo: Gone. After we cut down their forests. The ones
that survived we locked in cages for our amusement . . .
or used in experiments.

Unwanted Guests

Before we can set out, we're interrupted by an unwanted guest: Limbo.

"You're going nowhere," he says, dropping out of a tree. He grabs Gunnar and sets two of his handlers on Birn.

I reach into the emergency box. There should be one more thing in there—a gun. I pull it out and shoot the tree next to Limbo. He jumps about a mile. All of the apes stare at the piece of metal in my hand. They have no idea what it is.

"You saw what it did to the tree," I say.

Limbo's handlers take off. Limbo immediately lets Gunnar and Birn go.

He tries to kiss up to me.

Ari says that killing him will only mean that I've sunk to his level. She has a point. Birn puts a pair of shackles on Limbo. I'm deciding what to do next when Krull decides for me. He destroys the gun.

"Who would invent such a horrible device?" Ari asks.

Soon Daena and Ari are yelling at each other again. Limbo is shaking in his chains.

Thirty-six hours and I can't trust anyone but myself.

The next night we come across an ape camp. It's dangerous to get close, but they have something we need: horses. There's a river between me and my destination, and the horses will take us across. Of course, there's also a camp of apes in our way. I decide on a little distraction. I light one of the flares from the emergency kit. The stuff is coming in handy after all. The fireworks from the flares are like nothing the apes have ever seen. As they stare up, amazed, we hop onto their horses and head for the river. I light fires all along the way. We're almost there when one of the apes knocks Ari off her horse. I can't just leave her behind.

"You have to swim," I tell her.

"I can't," she protests.

"I won't let go of you," I promise.

We leap from the rocks into the river. Once we hit the water, Ari clings to me for dear life. Her claws dig deeply into my shoulder. But I barely feel them. All I can think about is getting to the shore. I focus every breath, every movement on going forward. I know the apes won't follow us here.

We make it across and find the others. They look surprised to see us.

Calima

The way to Calima is guarded by scarecrows that look like apes—frightening figures placed there to keep humans away. Calima is a holy place on this planet. Their scriptures say Creation began here, where the Almighty breathed life into Semos, the First Ape, in the time before time. The scriptures also say that Semos will return someday.

I am not headed to Calima because of the apes' holy writings. I am headed there because the Messenger's beacon grows louder and louder as we approach. This means the *Oberon* is close.

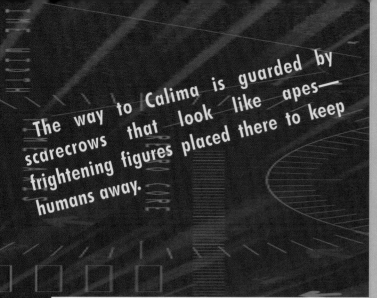

The way to Calima is guarded by scarecrows that look like apes—frightening figures placed there to keep humans away.

Calima is an eerie, silent place. Untouched. Uninhabited.

I see no sign of my crew, my ship.

"They're not here," Gunnar says, angry now. "They were never here."

The beacon grows even louder.

I see caves.

I head in that direction.

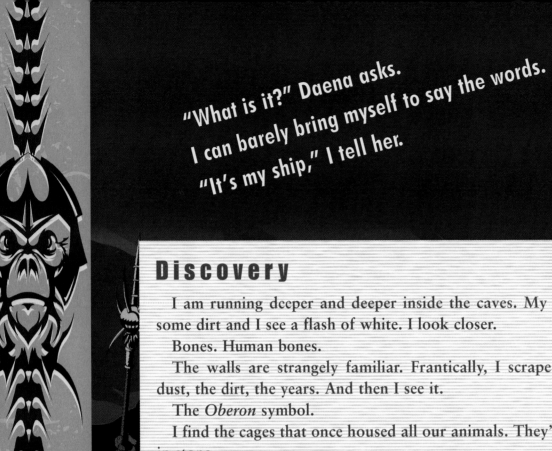

"What is it?" Daena asks.

I can barely bring myself to say the words.

"It's my ship," I tell her.

Discovery

I am running deeper and deeper inside the caves. My foot kicks some dirt and I see a flash of white. I look closer.

Bones. Human bones.

The walls are strangely familiar. Frantically, I scrape away the dust, the dirt, the years. And then I see it.

The *Oberon* symbol.

I find the cages that once housed all our animals. They're covered in stone.

The sign that once read CAUTION: LIVE ANIMALS now says only CA LI MA.

I go through the security door to the bridge. Dust fills the air.

I want to cry out. I want answers.

Daena and Ari find me.

"What is it?" Daena asks.

I can barely bring myself to say the words.

"It's my ship," I tell her.

"But . . . these ruins are thousands of years old," Ari says.

"I was here just a few days ago," I reply. I know I was.

I light up the control board. It says the date is 5021.946.

I need to know the truth. I open another control box to look for the visual log.

Is this something I really want to see? I look at the screen.

The Final Words from the *Oberon*

VASICH: We were searching for a pilot lost in an electromagnetic storm . . . when we got close, our guidance systems went down. We've received no communications since we crash-landed. This planet is uncharted and uninhabited. . . . We're trying to make the best of it. The apes we brought along have been helpful. They're stronger and smarter than we ever imagined. . . .

ALEXANDER: The others have fled with the children to the mountains . . . The apes are out of control. One male named Semos, who I raised myself, has taken over the pack. He is extremely brutal. We have some weapons but . . . I don't know how much longer we'll last. Maybe I saw the truth when they were young and wouldn't admit it. We taught them too well. They were apt pupils . . .

Then four large apes come into the picture. Grace and all the others are gone. I only saw them a day ago. But time stretched out for them. They are now all dead—victims of who knows what.

And it's all my fault.

Into Battle

I am amazed when I step back out of the remains of the *Oberon*. Dozens of humans I've never seen before are waiting for me. My story has spread through the village . . . now everyone wants to see the human who defied the apes.

"Send them back," I say. There is no way I can help them.

"Back where?" Daena asks. "They've left their homes to be with you."

I don't want to be their leader—because I can't promise them success.

But they're not going anywhere. They are behind me in whatever I do.

I now have my army.

Thade's army approaches . . . and we prepare for battle.

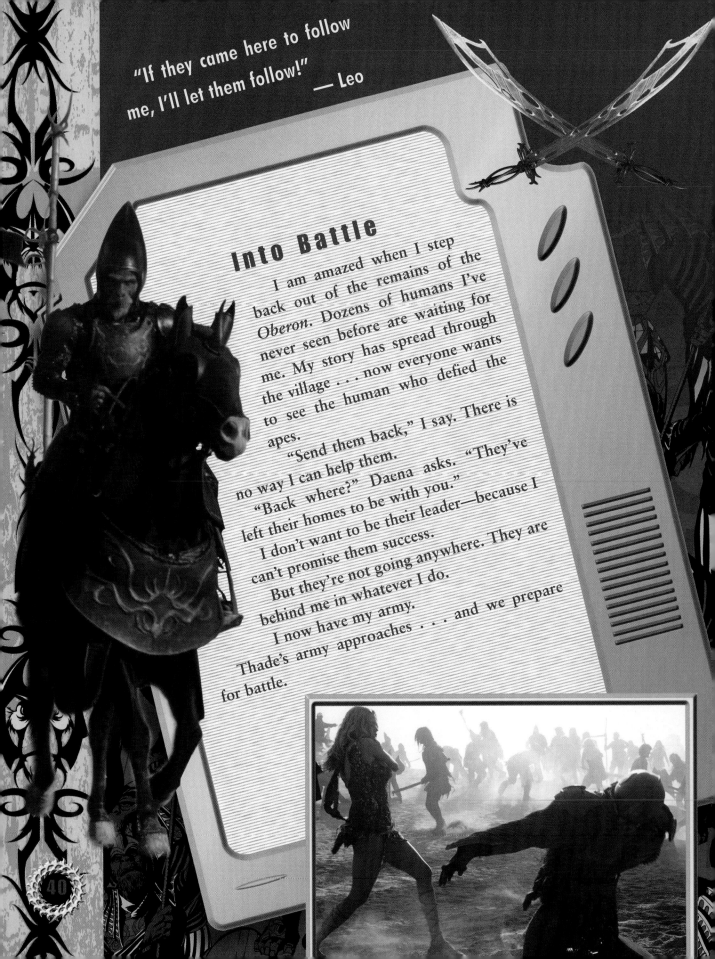

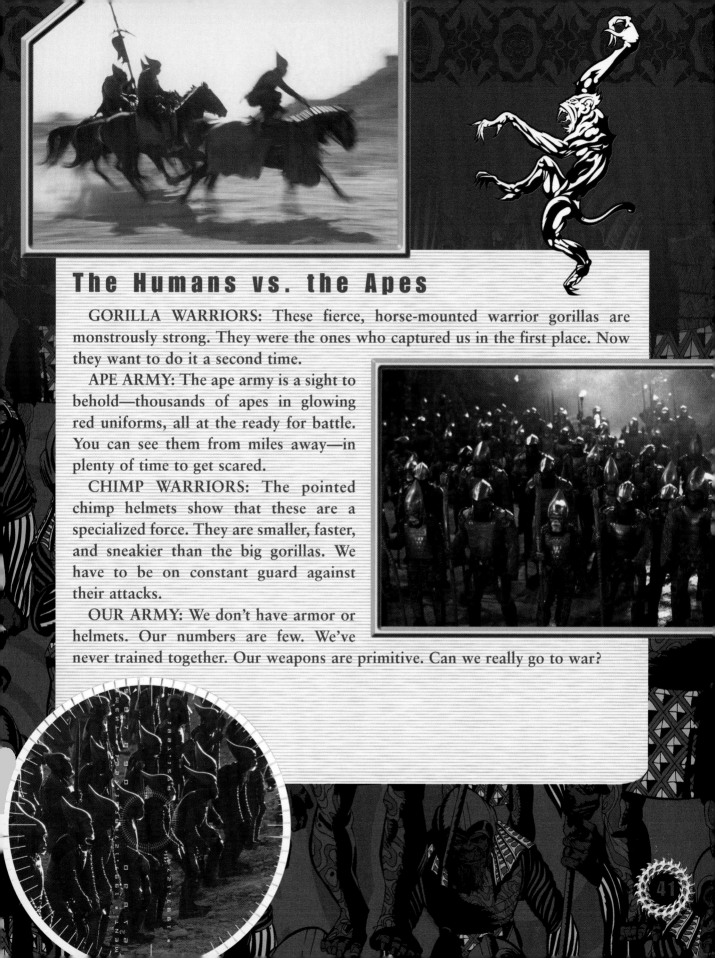

The Humans vs. the Apes

GORILLA WARRIORS: These fierce, horse-mounted warrior gorillas are monstrously strong. They were the ones who captured us in the first place. Now they want to do it a second time.

APE ARMY: The ape army is a sight to behold—thousands of apes in glowing red uniforms, all at the ready for battle. You can see them from miles away—in plenty of time to get scared.

CHIMP WARRIORS: The pointed chimp helmets show that these are a specialized force. They are smaller, faster, and sneakier than the big gorillas. We have to be on constant guard against their attacks.

OUR ARMY: We don't have armor or helmets. Our numbers are few. We've never trained together. Our weapons are primitive. Can we really go to war?

> "I am tired of this human. Attack!"
> — Thade

Attack!

I come up with a plan. We lure the apes toward the back of the *Oberon*.

When they're in range, I fire the engines and release a thrust of fire. The apes don't know what hit them. My side is energized, roaring back at the apes when they threaten us. For the first time in a long time, the apes are feeling fear.

Thade charges into the crowd, prepared for his final attack. They're all after me now. I dodge spears and nets. Tival isn't as lucky—the apes get to him and throw him from a cliff. Daena is knocked off her horse and Ari comes to her rescue. Krull faces off against his old foe Attar in a fierce battle of will and strength. And he loses.

Thade rushes at me. We fight, hand-to-hand, man against ape. I am too tired, lightweight, out of my league. The ape gains the upper hand. I dodge some of his attacks, then he hits me square-off. He prepares for the killing blow. Things are looking grim. Then something appears in the sky.

The Truth About Semos

Nobody recognizes the object hurtling toward us—nobody but me.

It's a pod.

It crashes through the clouds with a hideous boom and lands in a storm of dust and light.

The hatch opens slowly. The beacon inside the pod sounds over and over, a response to the beacon from my Messenger.

I know who it's going to be even before he appears. Pericles.

I am strangely ready for this, though I have no idea what will happen next.

"Semos!" Attar cries out, falling to his knees. "The prophecy is true. Semos has returned to us."

I run over to Pericles and give him a thumbs-up. He gives me one back.

Man, I'm glad to see him.

The humans cheer. The apes drop their weapons—except for Thade.

He charges at me again. He knocks Pericles out of the way, stunning the others, who think Pericles is their returned god.

"Wherever you come from, you're still just a wretched human," Thade growls.

He's not going to give up. He'll never give up. I know what to do. I lead him into the entrance of the *Oberon*.

I have to defeat him, once and for all.

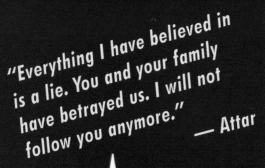

"Everything I have believed in is a lie. You and your family have betrayed us. I will not follow you anymore."

— Attar

Thade's Defeat

I think I have trapped Thade. Then Ari stumbles in and he takes her hostage.

"Let her go," I say. But it's no use. Thade now has the upper hand.

Attar comes in. I've sensed that he is more reasonable than Thade.

"Look around . . . this is who you really are," I say to Attar. "We brought you here. We lived together with you in peace . . . until Semos murdered everyone."

"Can it be true?" Attar asks Thade.

Attar hands Thade my weapon. Luckily, it's empty.

Thade orders Attar to kill us.

He doesn't move. He will not obey.

As Thade rants and raves, I back him into a corner. I activate the security door and it comes crashing at him. He tries to force it open. Attar moves in . . . and pushes him back.

"I will pray for you, my friend," he says.

There's no way out for Thade.

We have won.

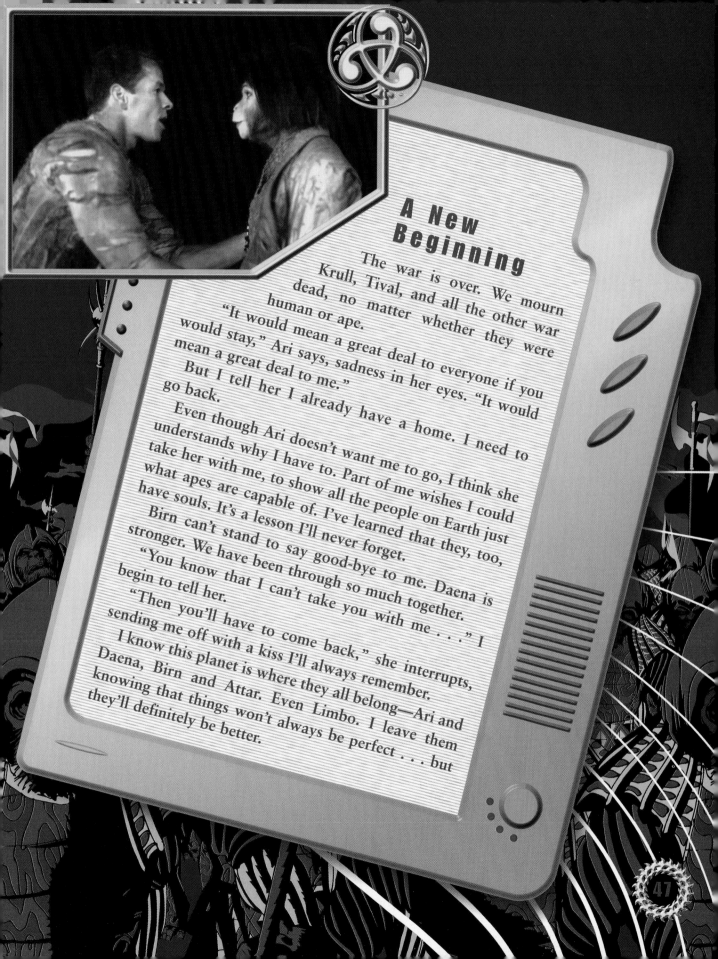

A New Beginning

The war is over. We mourn Krull, Tival, and all the other war dead, no matter whether they were human or ape.

"It would mean a great deal to everyone if you would stay," Ari says, sadness in her eyes. "It would mean a great deal to me."

But I tell her I already have a home. I need to go back.

Even though Ari doesn't want me to go, I think she understands why I have to. Part of me wishes I could take her with me, to show all the people on Earth just what apes are capable of. I've learned that they, too, have souls. It's a lesson I'll never forget.

Birn can't stand to say good-bye to me. Daena is stronger. We have been through so much together.

"You know that I can't take you with me . . ." I begin to tell her.

"Then you'll have to come back," she interrupts, sending me off with a kiss I'll always remember.

I know this planet is where they all belong—Ari and Daena, Birn and Attar. Even Limbo. I leave them knowing that things won't always be perfect . . . but they'll definitely be better.

47

Whatever storm that tossed me here is still out there. I have to take a chance that it can get me back. I take a seat at the controls. I feel the familiar lift of takeoff.

I am leaving the Planet of the Apes behind. My nightmare, my dream.